IT BLOWS MY MIND

Created by **Danny Marianino** and **Mick Lambrou**

ACKNOWLEDGMENTS

Layout by **Danny Marianino**
Cover and illustrations art by **Mick Lambrou**
Cover layout by **Jay Fotos**
Original text edited by **Matt Strangwayes**
Interior layout by **Micah Elliot**

Special thanks to **Krista Marianino** and **Roz Lambrou** for your patience while we spent way too much time creating this little universe.

ISBN: 9798406227558

TotalGavone.com and DannyMarianino.com

Created by **Danny Marianino** and **Mick Lambrou**

INTRODUCTION FROM THE AUTHOR

Have you ever been so annoyed by something you wrote it down? "Wrote it down" could mean something you wrote in a journal, texted a friend or even posted on a form of social media. Either way, it stuck out enough for you to take note of it.

Well, this happens to me all the time, except for some reason I really enjoy making lists and started writing down things that annoyed me almost twenty years ago.

I also began to slightly exaggerate them with explanations as to why I was bothered, and I found that adding context was often quite amusing.

That leads us to a character you are about to meet named Carmine. He's what I'd call an everyman.

I admit, we share a resemblance — similar hair line, fashion sense and ethnicity, as well as a hatred for germs. But as you read along and experience Carmine's daily escapades and dissatisfaction towards people, you too will relate to his frustrations. In the end, we're all a little bit like Carmine.

With the help of Mick Lambrou's illustrations and his quick and witty understanding of the book's concept, we were able to breathe life into Carmine and the cast of recurring characters you'll see throughout.

Especially that jerk, Troy. Trust me, you'll know Troy when you see his giant, smug smile.

Also, I'd like to note, if you read this book and find yourself asking, "Does Danny Marianino even like anything?" Well, I love grape flavored things, videos with puppies, chicken parm sandwiches, croutons, cigars, movies, my wife, a few people and hand clapping in songs.

I'm not sure what it is about hand clapping in songs that I like so much, but when I hear that tune *Car Wash*, you better move the fuck over cause this guy's hands are gonna be making some noise.

Enjoy -

Danny Marianino

OVER-FRIENDLY NEIGHBORS

I'm a firm believer in respecting others, but there is no chance I'm going to be your neighborhood friend. I have enough people I need to play nice with all day long, and when I come home from work, the last thing I want to do is get sucked into a conversation about some bullshit I could care less about. Do me a favor, don't involve me in neighborhood gossip. Yea, I know the Millers down the street need to mow their grass. Fuck them and their grass, I have to cook dinner and catch up on my shows. Here's something to gossip about; fuck the Millers and fuck you.

ANALYZING A DINNER RECEIPT

We all have that friend that has to itemize exactly what they got when a group of people go out to dinner. Now, I can understand that if you got an appetizer and drank water, the last thing you want to do is cover for the guy who drank most of his meal and ordered one of the most expensive entrees. It's your duty to have a clear financial understanding of the what you ordered and if you figure in a few dollars for the tip, you should be cool as a cucumber. It makes me insane when someone has to figure out exactly to the cent what they spent at a dinner with a big group of people. Just throw some money in already and stop being such a cheap bastard.

PEOPLE RUNNING MARATHONS

Here I am, I finally have a day off, and I'm excited to go out and do something for a change. Guess what, I'm stuck at the house because the streets in my entire neighborhood are in a lockdown due to do some bullshit marathon. Why can't these health people run in a fucking park, a track, on the fucking moon... I don't care where, just stop shutting down rural areas on a weekend. If you need to raise money for charity, you'd probably get more money if you went door to door and told people that if they just donated some cash, *you wouldn't* have to close all the streets down. I wouldn't pay to go out and jog around with a bunch of goofy suburban warriors, but I would donate a few dollars to not lockdown both ends of my street.

HOTEL PARKING AND RESORT FEES

What a bullshit racket! Many hotels charge for parking when you are already paying a fee to physically stay there. Am I the only one that see's that this is a shakedown? I'm paying to "park my ass" in a room. Now I am forced to pay for parking a car there as well? And what about the hotels that charge the fee even if you don't have a car? It's like if a car rental company charged you for a vehicle and then charged you another fee for the use of the tires. It should be illegal. What's next, charging me for bottled water?

THE TELLER AT MY BANK THAT LICKS HER FINGERS BEFORE COUNTING OUT MY MONEY

She does it all day, I always watch her to see if she does the lick before she counts for other customers. Just think of the plethora of stripper ass cracks that money's been wedged up in?

GREEN BEANS FROM A CAN

Unless you were broke and it was donated to you, why would anyone eat this when you can buy fresh green beans for the same price? I knew a guy that would chow one down in its entirety straight out the can. He loved 'em. Notice I said *I knew* a guy. I had to cut that friendship short.

PATRONS WEARING A BASEBALL HAT AT A RESTAURANT

It's alright if you're at a hot dog joint for lunch, but if you go to a nice restaurant, show some respect and take that hat off. That also goes for flip-flops. You think I want to look down and see those disgusting toes of yours when I'm eating a dish of vodka penne shrimp?

THE SOUND OF PEOPLE KISSING

Some people just make you want to barf. You don't sound attractive; you sound like Mr. Ed with peanut butter on his flapping horse gums before they added the voice.

WHEN SOMEONE SERENADES AN INDIVIDUAL IN PUBLIC

You are disturbing everyone around you. I didn't like that song when it came out; what makes you think I want to pause my conversation so you can profess your love? Save that shit for behind closed doors.

GUYS THAT MAKE UP THEIR OWN NICKNAMES

You can't give yourself a nickname. It's one thing to create an alias for professional reasons, legal or illegal. But you can't just start calling yourself "Big Dawg" because you'll look more like a big dummy.

THAT I SAVE EVERY PLASTIC CONTAINER

My cabinets are riddled with empty butter tubs and ricotta cheese containers. I have a quality collection of Tupperware, but I can't seem to stop hording a ridiculous amount of recyclable items.

RIDING HORSES

At this point why don't we give them a break? We have cars, there's no need to ride a horse. You think they want your big ass riding on top of them? Well, unless the horse is at the track, and I have a tip in the third race.

I WILL NEVER GET MY HAIR WASHED AGAIN

Unless you go bald, you will never understand the feeling of having your hair washed by someone at a salon. It's a significant loss in my life that I have not been able to move past.

CONSTANT COMPLAINING

Nobody needs that kind of negativity in their lives. Take that sour attitude and pickle puss of yours down the block. I'm rolling with a good vibe and you aren't about to spoil it! Got a complaint? Why don't you write a book about it?

WHEN PEOPLE CRITICIZE MY SPENDING HABITS

My folks had an entire room I wasn't allowed to enter, let alone sit on the furniture. We all grew up with that shit. The fact is, sometimes people buy stuff for their own inexplicable reasons. Don't worry about me, focus on your own bullshit.

THE OPENING CREDITS ON FORENSIC FILES IMMEDIATELY START AT THE END OF THE EPISODE

One episode rolls right into the next, and as quick as I am about to go to bed, I'm sucked into this crazy murder in Kansas City about people I've never heard of. I tell myself, "Ok, one more," but it always winds up being two or three more. I wish people would stop murdering each other, so I could just get to bed on time for a change.

WINDSHIELD REPAIR GAS STATION HUSTLERS

Listen, everyone has to make a dollar, and I respect anyone out there on the street trying to earn. But if I'm likely to have windshield coverage in my insurance policy, and I still haven't fixed my windshield, chances are I'm not going to let some fella off the street handle the job.

WIZARDS

What is it with people and their fascination with Wizards? They really are one of the shittiest fictional characters. Wizards always look like junkie homeless people. If I could do magic, my one spell would be to make all wizards vanish indefinitely. I'd follow up with fairies and crystal balls as well. All equally shitty. Just say the name Wizard. It's a dumb word. Wiz-ard. Just saying the name sucks.

NEW-SCHOOL METALLICA FANS

I was there in the 80s and it wasn't pretty! If you listened to Metallica you were considered by all authority figures to be either a druggie, a hooligan, a Satanist or a loser bum. According to teachers, parents, cops, counselors, and lawmakers, die hard metalheads who loved bands like Metallica were destined to fail in life. Most metalheads were unfairly judged because we didn't look like Zack Morris from *Saved by the Bell*. In truth it was the clean-cut kids that were going to clubs, sexually assaulting cheerleaders, doing ecstasy, fist pumping and stealing money from their parents. They hated the metalheads, and now all those same assholes love Metallica. They can all go suck each other's cocks and jam St. Anger. #RideTheLightingNeverForget

HALF OF THE PLUGS I HAVE ARE SO BIG THEY COVER THE OTHER OUTLETS

How many surge protectors do I have to buy to plug in like five things? Well, I'll tell you this, it's an obscene amount.

PEOPLE THAT SLOW DANCE TO AEROSMITH SONGS

That's the worst scenario ever. People do it all the time. I don't want to know those people, and if you invite me to your wedding and I hear, "I could stay awake just to hear you breathing," I'm out the door. Real fast.

BEING GUILTED INTO EATING FROM A POT LUCK AT WORK

No offense, but I don't know how you keep your house. Did you wash your hands between taking a shit and handling the raw foods you're about to feed people? I can't prove if you did or didn't, but seeing how you keep your desk, I have to lean towards the belief that your hands are shitty. Pot lucks should be banned in the workplace.

One day someone is going to unintentionally poison an entire office. If you have a cat there's a good chance there are cat hairs in your food. Your home-made chili looks delicious, but I think I'm going to pass. Forever.

THROWING UP

Bad enough you're feeling sick and horrible, but then you have to stick your whole head into a place you shit into. Come on, what's worse than that?

AUTO CORRECT

Auto correct never works when I can't spell the word, and it always gives me some crazy automated change when I can spell the word. For example, my big sausage fingers sometimes spell *new* wrong. It constantly corrects it to *nee'*. What the hell does that even mean? Help me spell *definitely*, not *defiantly*. If it's truly a smart phone, it would already know I never write the word *defiantly*. Just leave me the hell alone to my own big mitt misery.

#COWBOYUP

What a stupid hashtag and strange subculture. I find it so odd when I go to dinner or a store and see adult men and woman dressed like full-fledged cowboys. For that matter, the American Cowboys were total dicks to the Native Americans that were here before them. Now, if you work on a ranch, I can understand how some of that attire may come in handy, but if you live in North Scottsdale, drive a Mercedes SUV and dress up like a cowgirl while shopping at Neiman Marcus, there isn't too much of a difference in wearing Viking attire to the mall as well. Besides, those Viking helmets with the horns are way cooler than some Roy Rogers hat.

ITALIAN WEDDING SOUP

So, they threw a meatball in and called it Italian Wedding Soup. If this same soup was on the shelf at a grocery store, but had a wonton in it instead of a meatball, would they call it Chinese Wedding Soup? Some racist shit right there... It's good though, especially with some legit Parmigiano-Reggiano added to it. One thing is for sure, I've never seen this at an Italian wedding!

COMMERCIALS WHEN WATCHING A SHOW ON DEMAND

Ok, because I forgot to set my DVR to record a show I wanted to see, my cable provider is going to punish me by not allowing me to skip the commercials when watching a program On Demand? That is total bullshit. I demand you stop charging me so much, or allow me to skip ahead. Cable isn't free and by showing me commercials and charging me, you jerks are double dipping!

PATRONS THAT GET OFFENDED WHEN THE BARISTA CAN'T PRONOUNCE THEIR NAME

If your name is Czeslaw, don't expect that the kids making your coffee can say your name properly. What do you think, some teenager in Albuquerque knows how to pronounce traditional Polish names? Give them Charlie as a name to call out the next time and move on with your day, rather than give someone shit 'cause you are a big baby.

Even if the kid pronounced it as *coleslaw* when he called your name out.

BAD KARMA

Is it bad karma to wish something horrible on someone who sucks? Like a terrorist, a deserving criminal, or a neighbor that has been modifying the engine on the same Volkswagen Bug for two years and revs the engine all the time? I guess the question is — does wishing physical harm on someone with bad behavior gives me a pass on the bad karma? Seems like it should...

TRYING TO HAVE A CONVERSATION WITH A MIME THAT WON'T BREAK CHARACTER

If I have to explain this one, you deserve to be in this situation.

TOO MUCH PERFUME

When I go out to eat, I should not be smelling whatever garbage perfume you decide to bathe in while I am trying to enjoy a cheeseburger at Red Robin. I'm here for the bottomless fries, not to gag because you decided to cover up your stinky ass with way too much perfume. Screw you for being that person.

DON'T TAKE THIS MEDICINE IF YOU ARE ALLERGIC TO THIS MEDICINE

I get why pharmaceutical companies have to list all these possible crazy side effects that could happen to patients. Vision loss, heart failure, stomach bleeding, anal leakage... Whatever... But are we that stupid for them to feel obligated to remind us to not take something if we're allergic to it? Oh wait, I almost forgot, there are adults that eat laundry detergent pods.

REMOVING ITEMS FROM THE MICROWAVE EARLY AND NOT CLEARING THE TIME

It's just common courtesy, why does everyone not just do this simple thing!

FIVE THINGS THAT NEVER WORK WHEN YOU ARE IN A HURRY THAT WE ALL HAVE EXPERIENCED

1. Pay at the Pump: You have to run in the store and wait for some asshole to finish buying his customized lottery tickets.

2. Coupons Not Working: You are in the grocery store parking lot picking up your food and your one dollar off coupon isn't working, so the kid runs in the store to try and get it to work before you can tell him, "Fuck it, it's only a dollar. My Rocky Road ice cream is melting!"

3. There Is a Traffic Jam: Of course there is. Welcome to my life.

4. My Computer Wants To Do An Update The Moment I Turn It On:
This is pretty self-explanatory and as convenient as catching a venereal disease.

5. Your Friend or Relative That Won't Let You Get Off the Phone:
How many times do I gotta say goodbye before I just hang the fuck up!

HAVING TO SHIT AT THE WORST TIMES

There is nothing more annoying as having to take a shit when you're the best man at a wedding, pulled over by a cop, in a meeting with your boss's boss, three minutes from home, right in the middle of a church sermon or at some dirty bar with a bathroom that looks like they filmed the original *Saw* film there. Been there, done that.

THE FIVE SECOND RULE

Some filthy animal came up with this as a standard. Yea, I dropped a slice of pizza, cheese down on the boardwalk, but since it was only down for three seconds it's good to go. The germs and filth all know they have to wait five seconds before they can attack. Everything's all good!

BUSINESSES THAT DON'T OFFER FREE WIFI

If you want me to be patient while I wait at the doctors' office for an hour reading back issues of *Highlights* magazine, you better let me get on your WIFI. Who the fuck doesn't offer free WIFI in this day and age? Cheap bastards that overcharge you for their services, that's who. And don't give me the whole story about affecting someone's pacemaker. They would never be allowed to leave the house if that was true.

HAVING TO CLEAN UP SOMEONE ELSE'S PISS, SO THE PERSON BEHIND ME DOESN'T THINK I DID IT

I always end up doing this at a friend's home or at a small mom and pop business where some else might follow after me. I don't want to be known as the guy that pissed all over their toilet 'cause the person before me is a neanderthal.

THE CURSE OF OAK ISLAND

I know that Rick and Marty Lagina aren't going to find anything. They've practically dug up the entire island. The crazy part is, I got so excited when that Gary Drayton yells out, "Holy Shamoley it's a bobby dazzler," and all he found was a button. It's like an addiction and I can't stop watching. I get flustered week after week and I curse their whole crew, but oddly enough, if I had a few wishes one would be that these two lunatics find the gold.

SOCIAL MEDIA BREAKDOWNS WHEN A CELEBRITY PASSES AWAY

Don't act like you were devastated to find out Mickey Rooney died. He was 93 years old. You didn't know him and Mickey Rooney sure as shit didn't give a fuck about you either.

THE "CAN YOU HEAR ME NOW?" GUY SWITCHED TEAMS

Everyone needs to work, but come on buddy, have a little dignity. For years you told me the other phone company was the best, but since you needed work I'm supposed to believe the new one you're getting paid to brag about is better? That's a move you'd expect to come from a sidekick in a bad action film. What's next, Flo throws out the Name Your Price Tool and starts doing those Mayhem accident commercials?

OLD ROSE IN TITANIC

You have to respect the film *Titanic*, as epic as it was, especially for 1997. But come on, Old Rose throws that jewel over the ship at the end? The jewel is probably worth millions and her granddaughter could have lived an amazing life. But instead she wanted to give it to the ocean in tribute to Jack Dawson. Who, I should remind you, she didn't share the float with, and he froze to death. But yea, throw your money away. It seemed like her granddaughter was taking care of her, but Old Rose didn't give a shit.

BLOWING OUT THE CANDLES

I always wondered what your Aunt Helen's saliva tasted like. Those ninety year old yellow teeth and that mustache mixed with a strong spray of spit is a combo no one should endure, let alone all her relatives. Can we stop blowing out these bullshit candles already? Wishes don't come true.

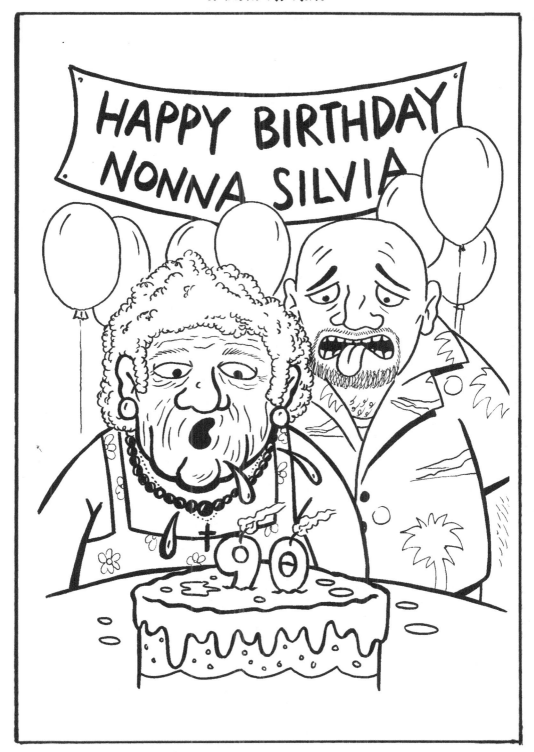

KAYNE WEST INTERVIEWS

Have you ever listened to that guy go on and on about the most insane shit, and the person conducting the interview just sitting there accepting it like it's the word of God? Some of the statements he makes would get you and I both locked up for being looney. Once, I heard him say he invented leather pants. Mötley Crüe never wore them ever; it was Kanye that actually invented it. It's not that I don't like what Kayne says, his interviews are slightly entertaining to some degree. He is a wild card, you can never predict what kind of wacky shit he is going to say. What gets me crazy the fact that not one interviewer has the balls to ask him, "Slow down, fella. What the fuck are you trying so actually say?"

THE ITALIAN GOODBYE

It's my own fault, but I have to say goodbye to everyone in a room when I leave. Everyone. I'm so annoyed with myself when it's time to leave a party. Then, sometimes, I say goodbye twice to the same person after I made my rounds because that first or second person I already said goodbye to is by the door. It's unreal, the Italian Goodbye makes me so angry.

'DONATE TO A CAUSE' REQUESTS FOR SOMEONE'S BIRTHDAY ON SOCIAL MEDIA

Honestly, I wasn't planning on buying you a birthday present. I just wanted to be nice and wish you a happy birthday on your page. Just a quick Happy B Day message. Instead, you had to make this big thing about it where I ended up getting multiple messages informing me I still had time to donate some money to whatever the fuck you thought was so important. Guess what, I blocked and deleted you. Hope you enjoyed your present-less birthday!

ONLINE MOTIVATIONAL QUOTES

I literally have one motivation when I see people post recycled quotes on social media, and that is to block the shit out of them as well.

WHY A CAR CAN BE SILENT BUT EVERY DENTIST TOOL HAS TO RUN AT A VOLUME THAT IS OBSCENE

Seriously, I don't know if my car is even running sometimes. Meanwhile, every tool at my dentist's office sounds like *Spinal Tap* turned their shit up to eleven. Sure, they're in your mouth, but I can't understand why one of these pharmaceutical companies can't fix this ridiculous issue.

PINEAPPLE JUICE IN A METAL CAN

These morons need to get their shit together. Pineapple juice is constantly sold in a metal can, but when you open it the old school way with the point on a can opener, you can't shake it up again. You have to shake pineapple juice, it separates. Put it in a bottle already and stop aggravating the world.

WET HAIR WILL GET YOU SICK

Who comes up with this nonsense and why do people keep repeating it? Fuck, I don't even know why I even give a shit, I've been bald since my twenties.

YOUR BEST FRIEND ATE YOUR CHICKEN PARM

I really went off the rails on one of my closest buddies because he ate my chicken parmesan hero I was saving for dinner. I may have overreacted a little, and later I apologized. Fast forward a few months, and he ate my cheesesteak sandwich that someone picked up and carried on an airplane from Philly to Phoenix for me. I never let him live that down, but he always checks now before he eats my sandwiches!

WE'RE SORRY TO SEE YOU GO

Here is the deal, I never came in the first place. But somehow, I ended up on your mailing list for a walk-in bathtub or a hair treatment plan. And to throw more gasoline on the fire, when I go to unsubscribe, I have to go to some strange website that seems like a security risk to get you to unsubscribe me for something I never asked for. It all seems very logical!

PAYING IT FORWARD

Sure, it's a nice thing to do, but when does the madness end!?

MY WIFE SCREAMS BLOODY MURDER WHEN SHE SEES A BUG

There could be a little cricket on the floor and you would think Freddy Kruger jumped out from behind a closet waving those fingernails around by the way she's screaming. She's going to send me into cardiac arrest with all this racket.

DO YOU WANT TO HOLD MY BABY?

The answer is no.

RESTAURANT CONDIMENT CONTAINER FILTH

Think about how filthy those bottles are, sitting on the table while family after family spreads their DNA all over them. Dirty hands, sneezing children, coughing old people, boogers... shall I continue? Most restaurants never clean those containers between customers and they actually just refill them rather than bring a new bottle when it's empty. Someone might as well just jerk off and shoot a big load all over the bottle and bring the variety count from 57 to 58.

DRINKING WATER FROM A COFFEE CUP

I would prefer to scoop water with my hand from a puddle than drink a glass of water out of a ceramic coffee cup. I don't know why I hate it so much, but I do, and many other civilized individuals share the same disgust. It's such a dumb thing, but it is definitely a thing.

CARDS OR INVITATIONS THAT INCLUDE CONFETTI OR GLITTER

I don't understand it. Someone sends you a card, it's a nice thing, but they stuff it with a bunch of garbage that will either fall all over your floor or your lap. Now you got to grab a vacuum, maybe change your slacks... You just defeated the entire purpose of the card by upsetting me.

WEATHERMEN SAYING THERE'S A 50% CHANCE OF SHOWERS

Just say you don't know if it's going to rain or not because saying there is a 50% chance is really the same thing.

PEOPLE WHO LOVE WOODY ALLEN MOVIES

It really takes a special sort of someone these days to recommend a Woody Allen movie. Well, maybe *Broadway Danny Rose*...

THE WAX ON BRIE CHEESE

I love the taste of Brie Cheese, but that wax around it is a total pain in the ass. I don't have the patience to cut it off. It's like the cheese industry hates Brie and is purposely trying to sabotage it. I am not sure why this wonderfully delicious soft cheese cannot be sold without a shitty wax like that funny cow cheese.

UNWRAPPED DINER MINT BOWLS

Do you remember going to a diner, and at the register they had those mint bowls that every Tom, Dick and Harry put their filth covered hands in? I do, and the amount of infections growing in those bowls still haunt my dreams.

DEAD AT 68

I find this sort of headline very aggressive. I feel like when I say someone is "dead," I'm saying it in a forceful, explanatory way. But, when I say someone passed away, I'm saying it in a more compassionate manner. Whenever a celebrity of any sorts dies, it's always 'DEAD at 62.' TMZ busts out a headline like '*Friday* Star Tommy 'Tiny' Lister Dead at 62.' It totally bums me out. That really needs to change out of respect for the family, instead of being like, "He's Dead MOTHERFUCKER!"

PUTTING LEMON IN MY GLASS

I like lemon with my water, but I didn't ask you to take your dirty piss covered hands and put them in the same lemon container that other piss covered hands have been in and finger fuck my glass by putting the lemon inside the receptacle.

NEWSPAPER OBITUARIES

I'm obsessed with finding out how and why people died. Every day the newspaper has an Obituaries section where you can read about the wonderful families, accomplishments and special people in the life of someone who recently passed away, only to conclude that, for some reason... they died. It's like leaving out the final chapter in a book. An obituary is a death notice, so do the right thing and tell me how they died.

STAYING AT SOMEONE'S HOUSE

Have you ever noticed how you end up tip toeing around when you're a guest at a friend or relatives home? Let's face it, no one ever sleeps as good as they would at their own home or even a hotel. God forbid you wake up early and set off their home alarm system. So here you are, sitting in their living room in the quiet, bored out of your mind, because you don't want to wake their entire house up by turning on the television too loud. As you consider going through their cabinets to look for fresh grounds because you're dying for a cup of coffee, you make a mental note to not use too much toilet paper when you take your morning shit. Imagine asking for a plunger as a result of you clogging up their toilet and it permeated until 10am because they slept in. The whole thing is a nightmare.

PUBLIC BATHROOMS

Humans are animals, disgusting filthy animals. There is nothing worse than having to drop a deuce in a place you don't want to be dropping a deuce at. The toilet is always gross and the floor in front of the toilet, where my pants and shoes will be, is constantly covered in some other asshole's piss. Public bathrooms are a nightmare.

FANTASY FOOTBALL FANS

Sports fans are the biggest nerds around. They create a make-believe football team with friends and colleagues that has stats that change weekly during the football season. I can respect someone being passionate about something, but when you poke fun at someone for playing *Dungeons and Dragons*, remember, you dorks are playing a fantasy game too!

MY MOM'S LENTIL SOUP

She made it all the time and it was horrendous. But, my father liked it, so we had to endure this on a weekly basis. I used to call it Dirt Soup because it literally tasted like dirt. Now, my mom will tell you I always loved it, but she'll also tell you I'm the handsomest boy in the whole wide world.

SHARON STONE

I want to dig Sharon Stone, she seems like she might be a lot of fun. But she was so convincing as Ginger in the film *Casino*, I can't forgive her for what she did to Lefty.

PEOPLE THAT CAN'T RETURN THE SHOPPING CART TO THE RACK

Really though, how lazy are you that you couldn't just walk ten to twenty steps across the parking lot to put the cart back in its correct place? If I see someone do that and the cart rolls into my car when they pull away, I'll wait at that store every day for a month, and when they eventually came back, I'll pick that entire cart up and smash it into their windshield. Maybe being held responsible for this sort of deranged behavior will make people return the carts to where they belong?

WRITING A CHECK AT THE GROCERY STORE

People still do this and its mind boggling to me. Then the poor cashier has to scan this bullshit form of payment after the purchaser takes ten minutes to write it out. During this ridiculous process, all the other shoppers waiting in line have melting ice cream and crying children, and they just want to beat the traffic. But you want to write a check for ten dollars. Ten fucking dollars.

CHANGE MY MIND

This phrase is constantly used online when people make absurd comments and expect you to go on their post and challenge them. Comments like, *"Doc Hollywood* is better than *Back to the Future...* Change my Mind." How about you just go fuck yourself.

THE PARTY IS OVER, NOW SCRAM

How many times have you thrown a party and you have that one friend or even acquaintance that just doesn't know when to leave. Or, for that matter, they're a repeat offender. These folks, *Party Never Goers* as I like to call them, have a reputation for getting wasted, staying too long and at the end of the night when you just want to go brush your teeth and sleep off the spinning in your room, they want to tell you how much of a great friend you are. Meanwhile, your only thought is throwing this asshole in a car and shipping them to *who gives a fuck* somewhere else.

COLD FRENCH FRIES

Why do French fries get so gross when they get cold? They get mushy and soft too fast. I hold a lot of resentment towards the longevity of potatoes.

PARENTS THAT BRING A BABY TO A MOVIE THEATER

I get it, you have a baby and you must bring it places. I can understand a parent's frustration with a baby freaking out at a restaurant or even on an airplane. We've all been there. But if you bring your baby to see *Rob Zombie's Halloween* and the kid is screaming bloody murder the whole time, that shit is on you. Get the fucking baby out of the horror movie, or any movie for that matter. Rent a movie like a normal person or get a fucking babysitter. Put a titty in its mouth... just shut that little bastard up.

CHOPSTICKS

Why would a Chinese restaurant give me chopsticks out of the gate instead of a fork as a first option to use as an eating utensil? Do I look like a guy that has chopstick experience? Then, when I ask for a fork because I have no idea what I am doing, trying to pick up rice with two sticks, the employees give me nasty looks as if I'm a problem customer. How about give me the fork first, and if I am feeling like a big shot, I'll ask for chopsticks.

I ALWAYS STEP IN DOG SHIT

There's a whole wide world out there and plenty of ground to walk on, but somehow the universe has it out for me and magnetically pulls my feet into dog shit. Either that, or I just have a big fucking X on my back which stands for bad luck.

PEOPLE THAT CAN CARE LESS ABOUT THEIR LUNCHES

What's the story with these people that bring lunch from home to work and pull out a bologna sandwich? Are they married to someone who could care less about what others think of your meal, or would they just eat any garbage someone puts in front of them. Then, I show up with a whole meat and cheese charcuterie board, all separated so the peppers don't moisten the cheese, and you have the nerve to tease me about going overboard. Maybe if you weren't so uncultured and ate like a champ, I'd give you a piece of prosciutto, but now you can go kick rocks.

WEEKEND YARD GUYS

Saturday or Sunday mornings should be banned for yard work. I get two days a week to sleep in and I gotta hear a weedwhacker at my neighbor's house right outside my window. There should be a law against this sort of anarchy.

DOUBLE DIPPING A SIDE

We all have that friend that does this when we're sharing an appetizer. Well, I for sure did. But I stopped hanging with mine, and if you had any balls you would do the same.

MOUTH BREATHERS

Hot breath just pouring out someone's mouth that never closes. A constant stream of loud breathing that is so powerful you can feel it feet away. The Mouth Breather does exist, and if you cross it's path in the wild, I hope you take my advice and run for your life.

REPLY ALL

There's always that one person at work that has to do the reply all on a departmental email. We see you, and we know you have shit on that brown nose of yours.

WHEN FRIENDS OR FAMILY COME TO TOWN BUT THEY DON'T CALL ME

I don't know why this bothers me because chances are I didn't want to hang with them anyway. It's safe to assume I would not have even picked up the phone. But, I still get so mad when I don't get a call.

A SINGLE BOOB OR ANKLE TATTOO

Oh cool, you got a Tasmanian Devil or the forever symbol on spring break. Aren't you the rebel!

ALL CAPS NO PERIODS AND OBNOXIOUS GRAMMAR

WE HALL HAVE THAT FRIEND THAT WRITES LIKE DIS WITH ALL CAPS LIKE THEY YELLING AND SHIT YO U LIKE BANANAS CAUSE I LIKE THEM I WANNA BAKE A BANANA BREAD BUT MY GIRL DON'T BAKE U EVER EAT THAT DR HUXTABLE GOT LOCKED UP FOR REALS I SAW HE GOT PINCHED.

WHY THE ZIPPERS ON MY HOODIE ALWAYS END UP LOOKING LIKE A BONER

Someone with seamstress skills has got to be able to fix this problem because a stomach boner is not a good luck.

PHOTO RADAR TICKETS

If you're going to fuck me, at least come over to my car and play with my balls a little. Sending me a ticket in the mail is the equivalent to giving the waitress of a restaurant a healthy tip when your order is for takeout.

COUNTING A PREGNANCY BY WEEKS

Why do I have to be a mathematician to understand you're 4 months pregnant? I get it, you go by trimesters and shit. But I go by months, like the rest of the fucking world.

CAN I TALK TO YOU TONIGHT?

Guess what, nothing good ever comes from that comment. Most men or woman will spend the entire day thinking about what the other person wants to discuss. Is it *that* bad that it has to wait until tonight? What did I do? Is this the end? It's clearly bad, because it had to wait all fucking day long, and I just spent an entire day on edge thinking about how severely screwed I am when I get home from work.

That comment will not only ruin your evening, but your day will also be fucked. Then you find out some shit like, "I'd like to expand our cable package."

Next time you get a message like that respond with, "Yes, we need to talk later!" Then go radio silent all day. Trust me, that will put a quick halt on this text message ever coming your way again.

NOT SHOWERING BEFORE A BATH

I don't know if you actually understand that if you just hop in the bathtub, you are just soaking in your own filth? If I am going to take a bath, I always take a shower first. Sure, it sounds crazy, but I get all clean and then I go in the tub. Honestly, I know I am a few steps away from being a Sasquatch, and I'm guessing you are too.

SLURPING SOUNDS IN PUBLIC

I swear, we live in a society of pigs. Keep it down over there! I'm trying not to throw up while I'm eating.

RESTING BITCH FACE

Don't look at me like that, or I'll give you something to be real sour about.

THE INDIVIDUAL WHO SUES A BAR BECAUSE HE GOT A DWI

Stating that you were greatly overserved by a bar and hiring one of those ambulance chasing law firms because you can't assume responsibility for your poor decisions is weak. Should I sue the pizza joint down the block cause their wings got me fat?

SUCKING ON A CHILI DOG OUTSIDE THE TASTEE FREEZ

Could there be a more repulsive line in a song than that? Every time I hear this lyric my hate for Jack and Diane grows stronger.

THE DOUBLE BIRTHDAY PRESENT HUSTLE

We all know this one. You stop by your friend's or relative's to give them a gift on or around their birthday, and then they tell you they are having a birthday dinner a few weeks later. You know everyone is going to show up with a gift. So, what do you do, announce to everyone at the table you didn't bring a gift because you already gave them one, or do you bring ANOTHER gift? It's a hustle. And if you don't bring a gift to the party, you might be so weirded out after telling everyone about your early gifting experience that you wind up picking up the tab for the birthday recipient.

MY PENS AND PRINTER ARE ALWAYS OUT OF INK

I can never seem to find a pen in my house that has enough ink to finish the first word "Hello" in a letter. To add insult to injury, the ink in my printer is always empty. I barely use the piece of shit, and I'm always out of ink. The whole thing is a scam.

MONOCLE

Can you imagine, someone wore this silly visual accessory and thought their shit didn't stink? Well, it did, and so do monocles.

MOVIE TRAILERS THAT SHOW YOU THE WHOLE MOVIE

Leave a little of the film up to mystery. It's like some of these studios want to tell you Bruce Willis was dead the whole time before the movie comes out. Take it easy over there.

YOU CAN'T HOLD THE DOOR FOR ME

I hope one day you are being rushed to a hospital, and someone doesn't hold the door for you. Maybe then you'll learn to have a little consideration, you soulless prick.

MY NEIGHBOR WHO LEAVES THEIR DOG OUT ALL NIGHT LONG

I'm three houses away, and I can hear the constant barking, all night long, while we're inside our house. You would think this *bachagaloop* would do the neighborhood a favor and let the dog in the house already.

LITTERING IN A URINAL

Someone has to clean out your gum or garbage, so be a decent human and use the garbage can you fucking bum.

STUPID NAMES FOR CHILDREN

Seriously, there are so many wonderful names — relatives you could have paid tribute to, role models etc. With all that being said, you chose Marmalade for your daughter's name. When Marmalade gets stuffed in her locker, don't say I didn't tell you so.

BATHROOM IS OUT OF ORDER

Don't lie to me. You mean to tell me that your employees work eight hour shifts and hold it in all day? Trust me you cocksucker, I don't want to use your bathroom, but I'm asking because I'm at that point where I have no other choice. Sometimes it's not really an option. I'm not a junkie or a bum; I'm not going to shoot up smack or wash my balls in your sink, so tell your *out of service* story to someone else and give me the key before I take a tremendous shit right in front of the register. And when the cops come I'll tell them my brain was out of order.

DRINKING COFFEE FROM A GLASS

I may have mentioned drinking water from a coffee cup is a horrible experience. Oddly enough, I find drinking coffee from a glass just as nauseating.

SLOWING DOWN TO LOOK AT AN ACCIDENT

Slamming on your breaks to see an accident only causes another accident. We all know that you're no hero; it's not like you are going to stop and give someone mouth to mouth. So hustle your little ecofriendly car down the road and get out of my way. I'm too busy for you and your make believe empathy.

GRATUITY INCLUDED

Here's a tip, don't include the gratuity. Chances are I would have left you more if you didn't include it in the total. But now, you get what you get.

UNANSWERABLE QUESTIONS

Things like "Which came first, the chicken or the egg? When I die, and if go to Heaven (which is *also* an unanswerable question, but I'm keeping my fingers crossed about it), I have a ton of questions for God. He's in for it. I want to know about dinosaurs, Oak Island, the Bermuda Triangle, aliens... and I want him to replay everything I ever said to my wife that she said I didn't say. If God created Earth and man, he has to have an instant replay button.

BENDING OVER BEING FAT IS LIKE DOING CARDIO

When you're a heavy guy, just doing the most simplistic things like putting on socks and tying your shoes feels like you just ran around. Suddenly I look like Chris Farley on a Saturday night all sweaty and winded. The struggle is real.

VAGUE SOCIAL MEDIA POSTS

When people post stuff like, "Enough is enough" or "I give up," are they hoping I'll post on their comment for them to tell me more? I won't. I have enough problems, I don't need to beg you to tell me why the fuck you're being so dramatic.

A GREETING CARD IS $8.00

Seriously, that's an insane price. Is Hallmark paying out crazy royalties to people who write all that verbiage? Because if so, I am going to start writing poetry for cards like Mr. Deeds.

CROP DUSTED AT A STORE

Man, there's nothing worse than someone walking past you and dropping a fart in your path. I know, I've been both a recipient and a dealer in fumes. When I do it though, I look around to see if there's people in my line of fire, as if I am passing the blame. It's one of those things I think is funny when I do it to others, but I get pissed when I have to smell your brand.

WHEN SOMEONE READS WHAT IS CURRENTLY ON THEIR PHONE'S SCREEN WHEN YOU ARE TALKING TO THEM

It's the same as someone picking up a newspaper or reading a magazine when you're talking to them. No motherfucking difference. If I'm not that interesting, then just tell me to take a hike rather than waste my time. I might as well talk to a head of lettuce because you are clearly too focused on this week's edition of *Who Wore It Better* and haven't heard a damn thing I said.

DRINKING FROM WATER FOUNTAINS

When I was a kid, I would drink water from a water fountain. Now, the thought of water splashing into the mouth of the person before me and splattering all over the drain that I'm putting my face over is something that torments my soul.

THAT I OPEN CLICKBAIT EVEN THOUGH I KNOW ITS CLICKBAIT

The headline reads: *You won't believe what Jennifer Aniston wore to the Academy Awards!*. Well, I'm intrigued. Twenty five pages later I'm feeling ashamed because I still haven't seen what Jennifer Aniston wore to the Academy Awards. I'm such a sucker.

THAT GUY THAT EATS CHICKEN WINGS ON OUR BOWLING LEAGUE NIGHT

Each week this piglet is licking his sausage fingers covered in wing sauce, barely wiping with a paper towel between turns with an alley owned bowling ball. His saliva covered chicken wing fingers keep going in and out of that bowling ball and I cannot stop watching in disbelief.

Do bowling alleys ever clean the balls holes? I'm going to guess that answer is a "no," because most people don't clean the inside of their own belly buttons. Ponder that the next time you go bowling. And to think, you were worried about the rented bowling shoes being gross.

WAITERS THAT SIT TO TAKE YOUR ORDER

I have experienced this more than a few times. It really takes some serious onions for a waiter to just have a seat and take your order. You can't say anything either, because if you do, you'll get boogers in your food.

NOT REPLACING THE TOILET PAPER ROLL

It takes about ten seconds to do, and yet we can't all make the time to replace it. I say "we" because I am guilty of this. I've had to learn to live with this shame, maybe you can too.

INSIST THAT THE STAR WARS PREQUELS WERE BETTER THAN THE ORIGINAL THREE

And while you're at it, why don't you and Jar Jar both go fuck yourselves. "Me so stupid me so stupid!"

TAKING ADVANTAGE AT THE EXPRESS CHECKOUT

The sign says ten items or less, and if you sneak in with eleven, it's not that big of a deal. But, if I catch you unloading twenty plus items and you see me standing behind you with three, you better let me cut. Otherwise, you may get cut for real when you get to your car.

DOCTORS THAT RUN LATE

I've been to plenty of doctors that scare you into being on time by threatening to cancel your appointment and charging you for a no-show if you arrive at their office fifteen minutes or so late. Hey, sometimes you hit traffic, it could happen. But I've also sat in plenty of doctor's office examination rooms for extended periods of time waiting for those same doctors who can't make to my room in a timely fashion. Where's the justice in that, isn't my time also valuable?

ARTICHOKES

So much work, so little reward. If I have to work tirelessly to eat my food, I'll stick to crab or lobster, like a boss.

THE CAMPFIRE SMOKE ALWAYS FOLLOWS ME

I can never enjoy a campfire like a normal human because wherever I sit, wherever I go, and whatever I do, that shit always blows directly in my face. Even during a chill moment, I can't catch a break.

MIXING OTHER FOODS INTO A FOOD CONTAINER

I hate when the peanut butter jar has jelly in it and vice versa. Or crumbs in the butter, that's just disgusting. I wipe my knife between products to not cross contaminate my condiments. This is a civilized world, try acting civilized instead of like a delinquent.

EMERGENCY ALERTS BLOWING UP MY PHONE AT 2AM

Are you kidding me, is this really necessary? Anyone awake at that hour has their phone on silent to not wake the whole house up. But, it's the people that are sleeping that might have forgotten to silence their device because no one normal is calling them at that ungodly hour. Real talk — when that super loud alert goes off at some crazy hour in the early morning and people are sleeping, they aren't going to read the alert. Chances are, if they actually do read it, they'll forget about it in thirty seconds and go back to sleep. So rather than wake up the entire neighborhood in a panic, send an emergency alert at a decent time and let me continue to count sheep undisturbed. It's pretty obvious no one is going to be looking for that blue Honda Civic at 2am.

THEY SINGLE ME OUT AT THE AIRPORT

Whether it's my luggage that they go through and fuck up, or the extensive searches, I'm always getting my balls busted by the TSA. Then they're rushing me to put my shit back on and move out of the way. It takes a minute to put this all together, hold your horses.

WALKING BAREFOOT IN A LAKE

I hate that mushy feeling and not knowing what I'm stepping on. I would lose that television show *Naked and Afraid* immediately because I'd refuse to step out of the boat. Well, let's be honest, I wouldn't survive the show without my C-Pap Machine, my K-Cups, the ability to watch a movie, or if I had to take a shit and didn't have toilet paper. Plus, who the fuck wants to be naked with all those bugs? I don't like getting naked by myself let alone with a stranger and a movie crew. The whole thing is fucked. Honestly, I don't know how people can physically walk barefoot in any mushy feeling and non-visible body of water and be cool with it. Savages.

THE ICE CREAM MAN STALKS ME

When I was a kid, I loved the Ice Cream Man and I'd chase him for blocks just to get a *Flintstone's Push Pop.* But now, when I'm working at home and I shouldn't be eating ice cream, this fucking prick sits outside my house playing *Pop Goes the Weasel* for ten minutes every day waiting for me to come out and get a treat. It's like he is tormenting my inner fat kid.

HOT TUNA CASSEROLE

It's such a common American dish and it's so disgusting. If your family makes this, don't ever invite me over, because I'm betting you inherited the taste buds of a walrus.

NAME DROPPING

So you know Dr. Oz, whoop-de-fucking-do. You can suck my dick.

FRESHLY MOPPED FLOORS

There is nothing more uncomfortable than having to step over, or walk directly on, a freshly mopped floor. Especially when the person is still mopping, and you're the jerkoff messing up their hard work. Not only will they have to re-mop where you just stepped, but your shoes are now covered in whatever scum they were just pushing around. That mop is a cesspool of scum.

PEEL-BACK CANS

I hate peeling back anything metal. It's dangerous and easy to slice your hand in half. Why can't they just make everything open universally with a can opener and help keep our fingers attached?

ELECTRIC HAND DRYERS

Sure, it's better for the environment, but now I have to touch the grimy door to exit the restroom after I've washed my hands. You can guarantee there was a filthy animal that didn't wash his hands and put his dick germs all over that handle at some point before you or I used the bathroom. It's a vicious cycle, and without paper towels to use to grasp the handle of said door, I'm getting someone else's dick germs on my clean hands.

STANDING REAL CLOSE IN LINE

Standing right up my ass isn't going to speed up whatever we're both waiting for, so instead of breathing down my neck, why don't you pretend that Onyx is here and back the fuck up.

LETTING FRIENDS BORROW STUFF

You either never get it back or you get it back damaged. Either way, in the end you get the shaft.

USING A RESTROOM WITHOUT A BIDET

When the great toilet paper crisis of 2020 hit, I did what any logical person who shits like an elephant would do; I bought a bidet attachment. I got so accustomed to actually washing my ass versus smearing shit with toilet paper between the cheeks until I was completed, that whenever I go somewhere and they don't have a bidet, I'm miserable. To say my ass got spoiled is an understatement.

SOMEONE INTERRUPTING ME TO TELL A STORY THAT GOES ABSOLUTELY NOWHERE

I was probably telling a great story but you decided to cut me off to discuss some nonsense that wasn't interesting, nor had an ending that anyone even cared about... what is that?

BANDS THAT PLAY ENCORES

I will never understand the thought process of musicians. Playing an encore should be completely banned from music venues. The lights aren't on for a safe exit, so we know the band isn't done, but we all have to wait for you to come back on stage to play the songs we all wanted to hear an hour ago. This absurdity needs to stop.

PEOPLE THAT NEED TO FIND THEMSELVES

Everyone is always looking for the bigger better deal. Stop being so soft and play the hand your delt. *Find yourself...* get the fuck outta here.

AND THEN YOU SUDDENLY FOUND JESUS

I didn't even know he was lost! So, you spent your whole life being a scumbag, but now that you found Jesus you expect me to look upon you in a different light? Nope. That's his job. You're still an asshole to me.

THE RELENTLESS FLY

How come flies don't quit, they just keep landing on your body, busting your hump with no fear of death? At least a bee will sting you as a defense mechanism, but flies are the most fearless living pain-in-the-asses ever to coexist with humans. And apparently, they take a dump every time they land on you. Real cool.

STEVEN SEAGAL'S NEW ACCENT

I'm not sure what happened to Steven Seagal, but he suddenly started talking like a blues singer from the seventies, and it's making me crazy. There has to be an old friend in his circle who can tell him that talking like he's from New Orleans and wearing those traditional Chinese button-down blouses is a bad combo.

THE PHONE PHOTO SWIPER

You show someone a picture on your phone and then they start swiping through every picture like you just handed them a photo album. It's so invasive! Imagine you recreated that *Cosmopolitan* Magazine picture of Burt Reynolds laying naked on a bear rug for your wife. The last people you want to slide into that photo are her parents.

Not that I ever recreated that naked Burt Reynolds picture for my wife. Who would do something like that?

WHEN YOU GO SEE A BAND PERFORM LIVE, BUT THEY PLAY ALL NEW SHIT

Come on, we know you're probably exhausted playing those same hits over and over. But it's those hits that got me out of my recliner to see your show, not the deep tracks off your eighth solo record that maybe ten people in the audience are familiar with.

THE SMELL OF ASPARAGUS PEE

There is nothing more embarrassing than eating asparagus for lunch and taking a leak at work knowing that anyone at the urinals around you can smell that nasty piss coming out of you dick. The worst part is that it's one of my favorite vegetables, so I always piss in a toilet, not the urinal, on asparagus days. You know you're in for trouble when you eat a vegetable that has a name with variations of the words ass and gas.

GIVING SOMEONE A GIFT CARD AS A PRESENT BUT THEY NEVER TELL YOU WHAT THEY GOT

I generally buy people gift cards so I don't purchase some garbage they don't want or need. I personally think I'm a considerate gift giver. But you know what's not considerate? When the recipient of my generosity doesn't tell me what they purchased! How am I to learn what their heart desires unless they tell me what was purchased!?

WHEN YOU ASK SOMEONE HOW THEY'RE DOING AND THEY ACTUALLY TELL YOU

Clearly some people are not aware that the question is more like small talk. No one that you casually know wants to hear about your cousin's baby drama or your bunions. Keep those bunions to yourself.

BALD GUY SUNBURNS

You people graced with hair truly have no real understanding what it's like to get a sunburn on your head when your bald. Especially when you have sleep apnea and you have to wear a face mask that wraps around your head all night.

NOT LETTING ME OFF THE ELEVATOR BEFORE YOU GET ON

If you are in a rush to get in the elevator before I get a chance to exit, you're a real prick. Of course, there are two circumstances that are understandable excuses. An emergency bathroom run is one. Also, if you are about to consummate your new relationship or marriage for the first time, I get it. Honestly though, you're a prick.

THE WANNABE COWBOY THAT EATS SHELLED PEANUTS ON MY BUS

Is the bus ride featuring a rodeo or some kind of country hoedown? I know this Roy Rogers looking shitkicker sitting over there throwing shells all over the floor doesn't care, but some hard working individual has got to clean his mess up.

FAKE REALITY SHOW EXAGGERATIONS

For example, I hate when the cast members of that reality show *Storage Wars* overevaluate the prices on items they supposedly found in a storage locker. Don't bullshit me, I know that Radio Shack Realistic mid-to-late eighties stereo receiver isn't worth six hundred bucks. That bachelor isn't looking for love, he's looking to get laid.

THE INDECISIVE SHOPPER

I always get behind that person who can't make up their mind... staring at the menu, holding everyone up. Or, they need to try every sample offered. Don't try the chocolate, you obviously know what chocolate tastes like. Oh, you would like to try vanilla and strawberry? I would like to drive your head through the counter, but even I know what restraint tastes like.

NO WEARING WHITE AFTER LABOR DAY

Who made this rule? I'll wear white whenever the fuck I want.

IF THEY ARE ELECTED, I'M MOVING TO CANADA

Everyone's always full of big talk, but show me one person that actually left the country after a politician they didn't like won an election, and I will kiss your ass. Yea, I thought so.

TAKE OUT ORDER IS INCORRECT

How do you leave the salad dressing out of the salad when *all you sell* are salads? That's just one fine example of an order I received completely fucked up at a drive through. And for the record, I really wanted a sausage and pepperoni pizza, not a salad, but I'm trying to make better choices and you destroyed my evening.

HAVING TO BUY A SECOND ITEM BECAUSE THE VENDING MACHINE IS A PIECE OF SHIT

I don't buy too many snacks from a vending machine, but when I do it always jams up, and I wind up with two bags of chips. Then I eat two bags of chips because I have the self-control of a beaver.

I CONSTANTLY GET SPAM MAIL FOR THE WRONG DEMOGRAPHIC

I'm in my mid-forties, and I've been getting AARP solicitations, advertisements for motorized scooters, the reversable mortgage, info on that bathtub that has a door... When will this madness end? Slow the fuck down with the incorrect age group advertising already.

LEAVING THE TOILET SEAT UP

Come on, have some common courtesy, you fucking caveman.

STANDING IN A LINE BEHIND ME AT THE URINAL

If there is one urinal in a public bathroom, how come guys wait inside the tiny bathroom with that smell of piss and shit when they can easily wait outside? You aren't going to lose your turn, slow your role and just wait outside. Besides, you're giving me stage fright, bro.

THE ENDING OF ALF

Season Four ends with ALF cracking a code he receives on Willie Tanner's radio and discovers that two other Melmac survivors have been searching for him and are coming to his rescue. Alf and the Tanners go out to a remote location, and an Alien Task Force shows up and takes them all in custody. Then the show gets cancelled by a network that doesn't care about its viewers, and — that's the end of the show.

I invested in a total of one hundred and three episodes of ALF for that bullshit ending. It was more disappointing than finding out Kevin Arnold doesn't end up with Winnie Cooper at the end of *The Wonder Years*. At least they got an ending.

WHEN SOMEONE RESPONDS WITH "THAT'S WHAT YOU THINK"

Yea motherfucker, I said it. That's what I think. I don't need this aggravation in my life!

WHEN AN ACTOR IN A FILM HANGS UP THE PHONE BUT DOES NOT SAY GOODBYE

I'm very troubled that this little common oversight happens so often in cinema, but not in real life. Imagine if someone did that to you; I bet you'd be wondering, what crawled up their ass? I'm a big Pacino fan, but hanging up the phone without at least saying goodbye is his signature move. Pay attention the next time you watch Heat; you'll notice he does it the whole movie, and you may quite possibly go berserk just like his character. Bon voyage, muthafucka!

BITING INTO FRUIT

I hate the feeling of biting into a solid apple or nectarine. I always go old school with a knife and carve that shit up.

THE LADY THAT KEEPS PLAYING KRYPTONITE BY 3 DOORS DOWN ON THE JUKEBOX

Over and over with this goofy song, it's like she's putting us all through mental torture. I don't know who hurt this woman, but it's not fair that she's hurting the rest of the bar, either. I hope she moves three doors down and gets the fuck out of our bar.

PLEASE PRESS ONE TO SPEAK WITH AN AGENT

Please pick up the fucking phone! Hire a human you nitwit.

PEOPLE SINGING HAPPY BIRTHDAY TO ME IN A PUBLIC SETTING

What do I do, just sit there with a dumb facial expression and watch? Some people sing along to their own song and I find that really strange. So, you just have to sit there and smile like a dope. How about the people that break into that Stevie Wonder version and start clapping their hands and shit? And *He's a Jolly Good Fellow*, that song is for real assholes.

EVERYONE I KNOW IS A MEDICAL EXPERT

I'll just go to the doctor, I don't need to drink bone broth and add oatmeal to my bath, I just need to see an expert. What is this the middle ages?

CAN I ASK YOU A QUESTION

You just did. Can you go fuck yourself?

THE 12 DAYS OF CHRISTMAS SONG

Could there be a more agitating and redundant song. Over and over, the same shit list of birds. By the way, who the hell wants all that fowl as Christmas gifts for twelve days? Even back in the old days before cable and shit, I would rather have been gifted a loaf of bread and maybe one of those suckling pigs. All my life I thought *eight maids a milking* represented a bunch of attractive women that milked cows, I recently found out that Maids a Milking are a bunch of Magpies. Do you what kind of birds Heckle and Jeckle were? Well I do, they were Magpies. Who the hell wants eight of those wise-ass shit birds.

YOU'RE A NO-SHOW FOR AN RSVP

You gotta have some balls to RSVP that you are coming to an invite-only event and then not show up. I hope you ask me to RSVP to one of your events, because you can bet your ass I'll get my revenge someday.

IT'S PRONOUNCED VOZ

Yeah, well in New Jersey we say vase, and we were a state before California, so maybe you're the one that's saying it wrong.

GRANDPA JOE IN WILLY WONKA

The guy is bedridden until he finds out his grandson won a Golden Ticket. All of a sudden he magically climbs out of bed and starts prancing around like he's trying out for Black Swan. It always pissed me off, even as a kid. Imagine the smell with four old people sharing a bed, pissing and shitting themselves. Charlie should have taken his mother to the Chocolate factory instead of that bum Grandpa Joe, she deserved a vacation from that living hell.

SENDING MULTIPLE TEXT MESSAGES INSTEAD OF A LONG ONE

We all have that friend that sends a million messages rather than just lumping it together in one message. It's always a delayed message too, like an hour after I sent the original text. Of course, my phone is across the house, and I'm fixing something or stuck on the treadmill. I hear the phone chimes over and over like it's a dire emergency, and I stop what I'm doing to make sure someone isn't in trouble.

No. It was just these six messages saying absolutely nothing...

LOL
That's Funnu
I meant funny
stupid spell check
Were did you get that
Where

That was his last group of texts because I blocked him. There is no coming back from a blocked number with me.

PAPER CUTS ON MY HAND

I don't know why I always get them; it's not like I am handling mass quantities of paper.

THE GIRL THAT WEARS TOO MUCH JEWELRY AT MY OFFICE

Everyone can hear this female Mr. T with her one thousand bracelets clanging together and clunking the desk all day long while she's typing from across the building. She also smokes lots of cigarettes and puts on hand lotion all day. So the combo of hand lotion, cigarette smell, and all that Long Island jewelry banging around straight up sucks.

WHEN MY KEY SOMEHOW GETS STUCK IN ANOTHER KEY RING THAT'S IMPOSSIBLE TO REMOVE

How the hell did it get stuck in the first place? Because I have to be fucking Houdini to get it out.

ENTITLED PEOPLE FLIPPING OUT BECAUSE THEY DIDN'T GET THEIR WAY

I just let them have their way because murdering them because of their disrespectful behavior is worse.

I CANNOT FIND THE EDGE OF THE CLEAR PACKING TAPE

It's always fucked up and my tape gun is no help. Eventually, I end up getting so heated that I throw it out and start over.

KETCHUP ON A HOT DOG

Who am I to tell people what to eat? But if you put ketchup on a hotdog or your eggs, and you're not under ten years old, I'm gonna open my mouth about it.

CHARLIE POKED YOU

What the fuck does that feature on Facebook even mean, and why is this stranger named Charlie always trying to poke me? Poke you, Charlie.

NEW YEAR'S RESOLUTIONS

I made a solid one about ten years ago, and I've stayed the course. It was to not make New Year's Resolutions.

THE WORD MOIST

I find that the word *moist* is horrendous in almost every context. Practically everything that can be described as moist is on the edge of being extremely unpleasant and borderline offensive, and I'm hard to offend.

Here are a few usages of moist that are repulsive:

The towel is moist.
The croutons got moist.
My socks or sneakers are moist.
My gym bag is moist.
This entire bathroom is moist.
The carpet is moist.
That handshake was moist.
This bread is moist.
The pages of this book are moist.

You picking up what I'm putting down over here? There's nothing that can be described as moist that is appealing, outside of a tray of brownies or cookies, and even then I use the word *fresh* just to avoid the most hideous word in the common English language.

WATCH YOUR LANGUAGE

I cannot be bothered with worrying about which words are considered foul language. Who cares if someone says *fuck*? It's a word. It's not a derogatory phrase towards a race, that I can understand people being up in arms about. Who came up with the rules that a word is bad in the first place? It's like saying, "I am offended you said *carrot*."

HAIR CLOGGING THE DRAIN

Just looking at a shower drain covered in hair is sickening, let alone cleaning it when it's not yours. That's right, you can't blame that shit on my shiny head.

CANCEL CULTURE HASN'T CANCELLED ME YET

Please do. I'll sell a lot more books like Dr. Suess did, and maybe everyone will leave me the hell alone.

PUNK ROCK SINGERS WITH A FAKE BRITISH ACCENT

That accent isn't fooling anyone, so stop pretending London is calling and start sounding like you did when you grew up in Detroit.

TELEVISION COMMERCIALS BEING LOUDER THAN THE PROGRAM

I know they do this on purpose, and it's aggravating. Commercials always seem to be the loudest when you fall asleep. Suddenly you're awakened by a jingle yelling, "This is a cold call!" Damn you Ice-T and Stone Cold, damn you both.

INSIDE JOKES BETWEEN PEOPLE

How about you not do that in front of others cause it makes you look like a massive fuckface.

WHEN A COLLEAGUE HANDS YOU A CHEWED UP PEN

What are we still in elementary school? Stop chewing up your pens, and don't you dare hand it to me because I will throw it across the room. Buy some Doublemint already and get that pen that fell on the floor a few times today out of your mouth.

THE EMPLOYEES AT THE PRICE CLUB WHO ALWAYS ASK ME AT THE REGISTER IF I WANT A BOX

No, I want to hand carry all this shit to my car. All seventeen bulk items.

STICKERS ON HATS

Someone told me that people keep the stickers on their baseball hat brim as a sign of wear and tear. When the sticker wears off naturally, it's time to get a new hat. And here I thought the human race still had hope.

And last but not least...

THE FACT THAT I HAD TO WRITE THIS BOOK BECAUSE EVERYONE IS SO UNCIVILIZED

That's right, I'm sure there is something in here that you do. It's alright, as long as you learn from your mistakes. Or at least stay far the fuck away from me.

Keep an eye out for more of Carmine's
adventures coming soon from:

TOTAL GAVONE PUBLISHING!

Visit us at <u>TotalGavone.com</u>.

ABOUT THE AUTHOR

Danny Marianino — The New Jersey native is the author of *Don't Ever Punch a Rockstar A Collection of Hate Mail and Other Crazy Rumors* (DiWulf Publishing), *The Mega Book of Revenge Films Vol. 1 The Big Payback*, *The Belligerent Book of Movie Quotes* and more recently *To Make Matters Worse*, which is also available as an audio book through Audible. He has been a contributing writer for many different publications and various websites such as *Bullet Proof Action*, *Lunchmeat Zine* and ICanSmellYourBrains.com. Danny has also been a prominent member of the punk and hardcore music scene from his time playing in North Side Kings, and has been featured in publications such as *Decibel Magazine*, *The A.V. Club*, Vice.com, *L.A. Times*, *Phoenix New Times* and *Spin Magazine*. He has been featured on television networks such as MTV, VH1 and on TruTV. Danny also owns a clothing line called Total Gavone Streetwear.
Follow **@TotalGavoneClothing** and also **@DannyMarianino**.

Mick Lambrou — This Australian illustrator has worked with some of Hardcore and Punk Rock's most legendary bands, including NYHC Legends Agnostic Front, Madball, Murphy's Law, Sheer Terror, The Business, Subzero, Slapshot, North Side Kings and many, many others. Mick resides in Melbourne, Victoria with his wonderful, patient and understanding wife Roz and 2 young, cheeky little ratbag sons, Archie and Angus. If you are interested in keeping up with Mick's projects, be sure to follow him on Instagram at **@MickLambrou**.

Copyright © 2022 Total Gavone LLC